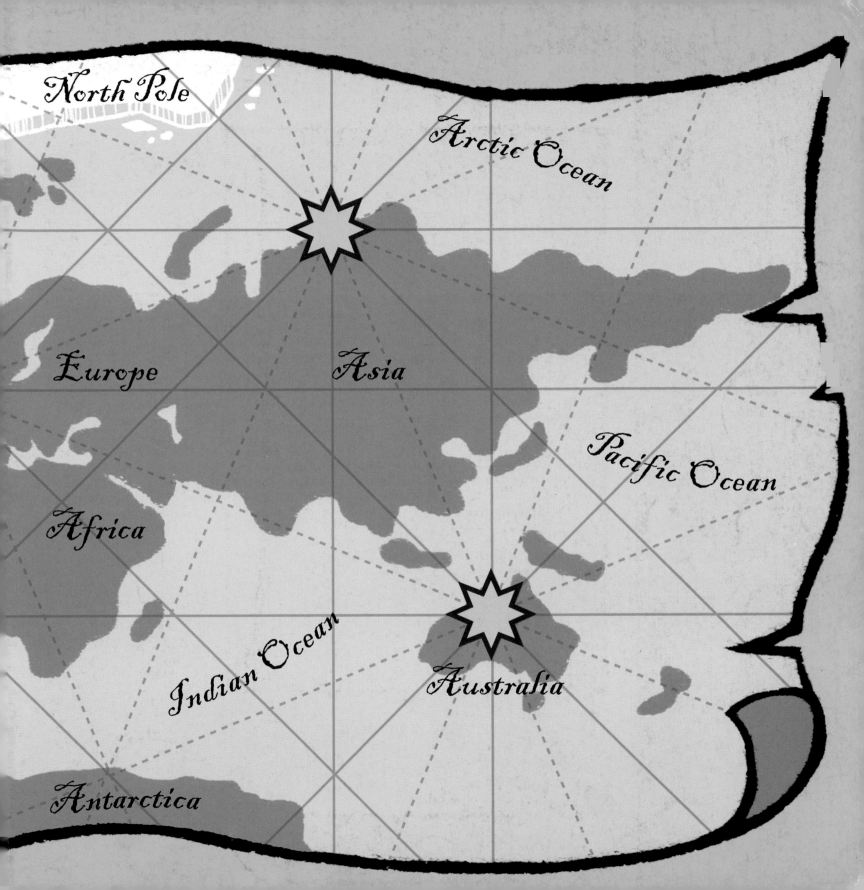

For Mike and Elim

Bloomsbury Publishing, London, New Delhi, New York and Sydney

First published in the United States of America in 2015
by Bloomsbury Children's Books
1385 Broadway, New York, New York 10018

This edition first published in Great Britain in 2015 by Bloomsbury Publishing Plc
50 Bedford Square, London, WC1B 3DP

Text and illustrations copyright © Salina Yoon 2015

The moral right of the author/illustrator has been asserted

A CIP catalogue record for this book is available from the British Library

ISBN 978 1 4088 6871 3

Printed in China by Leo Paper Products, Heshan, Guangdong

1 3 5 7 9 10 8 6 4 2

www.bloomsbury.com

BLOOMSBURY is a registered trademark of Bloomsbury Publishing Plc

Penguin's Big Adventure

Salina Yoon

BLOOMSBURY

LONDON   NEW DELHI   NEW YORK   SYDNEY

One day, Penguin had a big idea.

He wanted to do something no penguin had ever done.

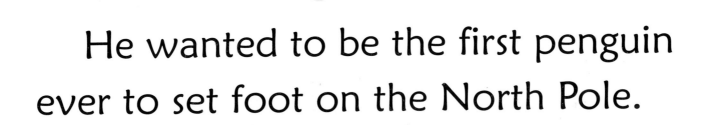

He wanted to be the first penguin ever to set foot on the North Pole.

Penguin planned and packed.
He rolled up his adventure map
and set off.

But before his first mile,
Penguin saw Emily sewing.

'This looks like a very nice quilt,' said Penguin, 'and the brightest I've ever seen!'

Before Penguin reached his second mile, he saw his little brother, Pumpkin, weaving.

'That is a fine basket, Pumpkin,' said Penguin, 'and the biggest I've ever seen!'

Right before his third mile, he saw
Bootsy braiding the longest rope he'd
ever seen.

Then Penguin set off for the other side of the world, while his busy friends worked on their own world records.

Penguin passed through his favourite places and visited old friends.

He had a whale of a time!

Finally, Penguin reached the North Pole.

I'm on top of the world!

Penguin threw confetti,

turned cartwheels

and planted a sign.

Penguin shouted, 'HOORAY!'
and it echoed across the ice.

Nobody answered.

Penguin was suddenly lonely and afraid.

Oh!

But he was not alone.

Penguin had never
seen a polar bear.

And Polar Bear had never seen a penguin.

It was scary.

Penguin and Polar Bear smiled.
And it wasn't so scary any more.

Together they went on a North Pole adventure.

built ice forts,

They went whale watching,

explored the Arctic Sea

and welcomed
more visitors!

We
missed
you!

Then it was time for the
new friends to say goodbye.

Penguin left Polar Bear his adventure map. He didn't need it any more.

Because the best part of
having an adventure is . . .

. . . coming home!

World Record

First penguin to set foot on the North Pole!

Penguin

Certified by ___Grandpa___

Witnessed by ___Polar Bear___

World Record

First polar bear to meet a penguin!

Polar Bear
_____

Certified by _____ Grandpa _____

Witnessed by _____ Penguin _____

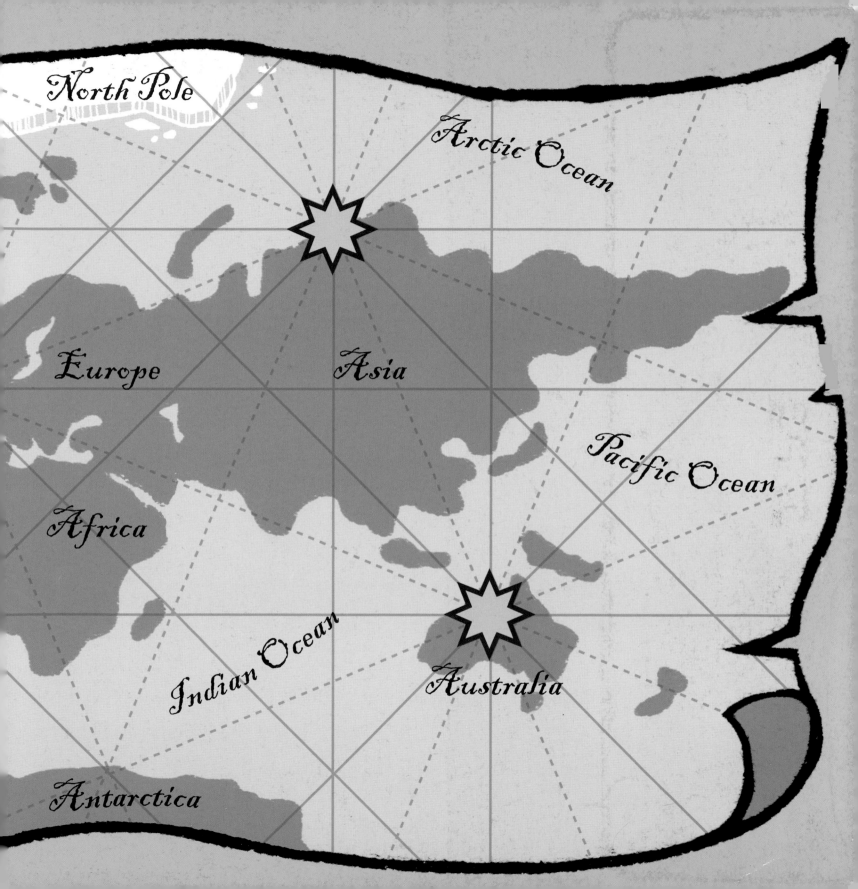